TERRIBLE NEWS

Corey watched as her two best friends climbed out of Mr. Grover's car. May stared straight at the ground. Jasmine looked as though she had tears in her eyes.

Corey dashed over to the back of the van hitched to the Grovers' car. She opened the door. It took only a second for her to see that there weren't three ponies back there. There were only two—and neither of them was Samurai.

She turned to her friends. "You forgot my pony!"

Jasmine shook her head. "No, we didn't," she said softly. "We went to get him, but . . ." Tears streaked down her cheek.

"Oh, Corey!" May said sadly. "Samurai is . . . *missing!*"

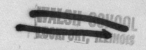

Corey's Pony Is Missing

BONNIE BRYANT

Illustrated by Marcy Ramsey

A SKYLARK BOOK
NEW YORK • TORONTO • LONDON • SYDNEY • AUCKLAND

RL3 007–010
COREY'S PONY IS MISSING
A Skylark Book / September 1995

Skylark Books is a registered trademark of Bantam Books,
a division of Bantam Doubleday Dell Publishing Group, Inc.
Registered in U.S. Patent and Trademark Office and elsewhere.
Pony Tails is a trademark of Bonnie Bryant Hiller.

ISBN 0-553-48257-2

Published simultaneously in the United States and Canada

Bantam Books are published by Bantam Books, a division of Bantam
Doubleday Dell Publishing Group, Inc. Its trademark, consisting of the
words "Bantam Books" and the portrayal of a rooster, is Registered in
U.S. Patent and Trademark Office and in other countries. Marca
Registrada. Bantam Books, 1540 Broadway, New York, New York 10036.

PRINTED IN THE UNITED STATES OF AMERICA

OPM   0 9 8 7 6 5 4 3 2 1

Corey's Pony
Is Missing

1 Time to Go

"Where are my riding boots?" Corey Takamura called to her mother.

"In your closet," Dr. Takamura answered. "Or at least that's where they *ought* to be."

Corey put down her riding pants and went to look in her closet. She moved a small pile of dirty clothes. There were her boots. She sighed and pulled out the laundry. She carried the clothes to the hamper in her bathroom. Then she took her boots and put them in her suitcase. She was almost ready, but she was sure she'd forgotten one more thing.

Usually Corey was very sensible and logical and could have found her boots without help from her mother. Today was different. Today she was packing to go to her father's for the weekend.

Corey's parents had been divorced for only a short while. She spent half her time with her mother, a veterinarian whose nickname was Doc Tock.

Corey's father lived in an apartment closer to town. He was a teacher at the high school next to Corey's elementary school.

Corey and her parents were still deciding which days she would spend with which parent. Sometimes, like when her mother was busy with moving arrangements, Corey spent a whole week at a time with her father. Other times, like when her father went on a trip to Mexico with his Spanish class, she spent a whole week with her mother. Usually, though, she liked to spend weekends at her mother's house. That way, she could be with her pony, Samurai, all day Saturday and Sunday. But this weekend she was going to her father's. Her mother had to go to a veterinarians' convention. She was going to give a speech.

Corey was excited for her mother, but it was confusing for her. Since she would be with her father for the weekend, she'd be going to Horse Wise, her Pony Club meeting,

Corey's Pony Is Missing

from his apartment, and she needed her riding clothes.

"My hat! That's what I forgot!" she said out loud, though there was nobody there to hear her. Her mother was busy in her own room with her own packing.

Corey found her riding hat in her closet. That went into her suitcase, too. She started to close the suitcase. Then she remembered something else—rubber bands. She was growing her hair and it was almost long enough for a ponytail. Just in case it grew enough over the weekend, she wanted to be sure to have the rubber bands. In a minute they were in her suitcase, too. She snapped it shut. There was one more thing she had to do. She had to say good-bye to Samurai.

*   *   *

"Weekends are much more fun when Corey is here," May Grover said to Jasmine James. May and Jasmine were Corey's neighbors. They lived on either side of Corey's house. Corey had only lived there a short while, but already the girls were best friends. They were very different, but they had some very important things in common.

3

Pony Tails

First, they were the same age, so they were all in third grade. They were in different classes, but they went to the same school. More important, they were each pony crazy, and each had her own pony. That was why they called themselves the Pony Tails. It was like a club for best friends who loved ponies.

May always said exactly what was on her mind. Sometimes that got her into trouble. She could be stubborn, too. But she knew a lot about ponies. Her pony had a sweet yellow coat that matched his sweet disposition. May had named him Macaroni because he was the color of macaroni and cheese. May thought he was the sweetest pony in the whole world.

Jasmine's pony was named Outlaw. He could be frisky and naughty. Sometimes he nipped and bucked. Jasmine called him Outlaw because his whole face was white. It looked like the kerchief outlaws pulled up on their faces when they robbed a stagecoach. Sometimes she thought he was almost naughty enough to do something like that, too! Jasmine loved Outlaw more than anything—maybe because he was so different from her.

Corey's Pony Is Missing

Corey's pony was named Samurai after the crescent-shaped blaze on his face. It looked like a samurai sword. Samurai was a young pony and less well trained than Outlaw and Macaroni. He was very smart, but he had a lot to learn. It had taken him a long time to adjust to his new home when Corey and her mother had moved. Now both he and Corey felt at home in their new place.

"Come on, May," Jasmine said. May was still upset about Corey's going away for the weekend. "Corey goes to her father's every week." The two girls were in Outlaw's stable, giving him some fresh hay.

"But this time she's going for the whole weekend," May pointed out. "We were going to practice the riding exercises together after school tomorrow."

"It's just for a few days," Jasmine told her friend. "Corey will be back on Sunday. Maybe we'll have time to practice then. Besides, we'll see her at school tomorrow and at Pony Club on Saturday."

"I know," said May. "Sometimes it just seems strange. I mean she's our best friend, but we don't know anything about her other life."

Jasmine nodded. It was true. The girls only saw Corey at her mother's house or at school. They had never been to her father's apartment. They didn't even know where it was.

"I bet it's a nice apartment," Jasmine said. She was trying to comfort her friend. "And Corey probably has a great bedroom. I can see it now. It's got pink flowered wallpaper and matching curtains."

May knew Jasmine was describing her own dream bedroom.

"Nah, plain colored walls so she can cover them with horse posters," May said.

This time Jasmine knew May was describing her own bedroom.

"Maybe she even has a pink bedspread," said Jasmine.

May rolled her eyes. "Don't you like anything besides pink, Jasmine? I hope Corey's room is blue with a big bookshelf for all her horse books."

"And a big table for all her model horses," said Jasmine.

"Wait a minute! You're the one with all the model horses," May reminded her friend.

"And you're the one with all the books about horses," Jasmine said.

Corey's Pony Is Missing

May laughed. "I guess we're both thinking about what *we'd* like, not what Corey likes."

Jasmine smiled. "Let's go see Samurai," she said. "We both know for sure that she likes Samurai, right?"

"Definitely."

May closed Outlaw's stall, and Jasmine snapped the lock shut tight. They turned out the stable light and walked over to Corey's house. The Pony Tails often visited each other's ponies.

Samurai was in his stable. So was Corey.

"We thought you'd be gone," May said.

"Almost," said Corey. "Dad'll be here in a minute. I just wanted to say good-bye to Samurai first."

"We're going to miss you," May blurted out.

"I wish I could be here to practice with you two on Sunday, but it's impossible," said Corey.

"Is your dad's apartment nice?" May asked.

"Of course it is," said Corey. "I have my own bedroom there. Dad's been decorating it just for me."

It was another thing they didn't know about Corey! May and Jasmine exchanged looks.

"Where is your dad's apartment?" Jasmine asked as she handed Corey some hay for Samurai.

"It's on Shelley Lane," Corey said. "It's across from the restaurant."

"The hamburger place?" May asked. She was trying to picture Shelley Lane in her mind.

"No, they have pizza," said Corey. "We usually go there at least once a week." She tucked the hay into Samurai's manger. He munched happily.

"I didn't think you liked pizza," said Jasmine.

"This is really good pizza," said Corey.

"Oh," said May. She couldn't picture Corey eating pizza. It made Corey's life at her father's house seem even stranger.

May patted Samurai. He barely noticed because he was so content to chew on the hay. May barely noticed she was patting him either. She was too busy thinking about Corey at her father's house.

"We're going to miss you when we go riding over the weekend," said Jasmine, changing the subject.

"We'll feed Samurai. We promise," said May.

Corey's Pony Is Missing

"Thanks." Corey smiled.

"And we'll bring him to Horse Wise on Saturday," Jasmine added.

"Definitely," May said. "You have nothing to worry about."

"I never worry when my two best friends are looking after my pony," said Corey.

May closed the door to Samurai's stall. Jasmine latched it tightly.

"Corey!" Doc Tock called from the house.

Corey didn't want to leave, but she knew it was time. "Dad's here," she explained.

"Have a good time," Jasmine told her.

"Bye," said May. "See you tomorrow at school."

"See you," Corey said.

She was talking to her friends, but she was looking at Samurai. He looked up at her and blinked. He seemed surprised that she was leaving while May and Jasmine were still there.

"Don't worry, boy," Jasmine told him. "She'll be back before you know it."

Samurai stared at Corey as she walked out of the stable. When she passed through the entryway, he stuck his head out over his stable door and watched her until she disappeared into the house.

Pony Tails

"It's okay, Sam," Jasmine said softly. "You'll see her again soon."

He snorted and stomped his feet.

May patted Corey's pony. "That's right, boy," she added. "You and Corey will be riding together again before you know it."

2 Corey's Other Home

Corey dashed through the house. She gave her mother a hug. Then she picked up her suitcase.

"Good luck with your speech," Corey said.

"Thanks," Dr. Takamura said. "I'll bring you a present from New Orleans. Now, don't forget, if you need anything from the house, Jack will be here in the daytime." Jack was Doc Tock's student assistant. He would look after the patients that were staying in Doc Tock's infirmary while she was gone. He'd also feed Samurai in the mornings.

Corey trusted Jack, though she didn't know him very well. He never said much to people. But when it came to animals, he talked constantly. And no matter what he said, the animals seemed to understand him. Doc Tock said he'd make a fine veterinarian one day.

"Okay, Mom," Corey said. Then she took a deep breath and turned to the door. The hardest thing about having divorced parents was saying good-bye to one and hello to the other.

Her father was waiting at the curb. Mr. Takamura was a short man with straight black hair. Some of his students at Willow Creek High School thought he was a strict man. Corey knew better. She thought her father was the gentlest, most understanding man in the world.

Now he was standing next to his car with his arms out.

"Hi, sugar!" he called.

"Daddy!" Corey answered. She ran over to him and dropped her suitcase by the car before she jumped into his waiting arms.

The hard part was over. She was with her father now.

A few seconds later her suitcase was tucked into his trunk, and they drove away from the curb.

"I didn't get to go shopping," her father explained. "Do you mind eating out at Pat's?"

"Not at all," Corey said. "I love Pat's pizza. In fact, it's the only pizza I *do* like." Then she

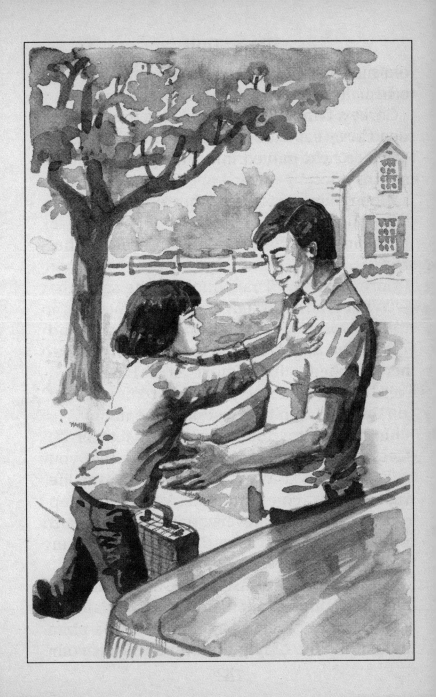

told him that her friends had been surprised to hear that she ever ate pizza.

Corey's father thought that was funny. He'd seen Corey eat a lot of pizza at Pat's pizza parlor since he'd moved into the apartment two months ago.

When they got to Pat's, they ordered a pepperoni pizza and two sodas.

"Tell me about your friends," Corey's father said.

Corey smiled. "That's funny," she said.

"What is?" he asked.

"They were just asking me about you and your apartment," Corey replied. Corey's father laughed. "It's almost as if I lead two lives," she went on. "They don't know about you and you don't know about them."

Mr. Takamura took a sip of his soda. "I guess it seems that way sometimes—that you have two lives, I mean. But it's really one life with different compartments. When you stop to think about it, everybody has different compartments, don't they? For instance, your teachers may not know about your pony."

"Sure they do. I talk about horses all the time at school," Corey said.

"All right, then something else," Mr. Takamura said. "They don't know what your home is like and you don't know what their homes are like. Your riding instructor, what's his name, the man who runs Pine Hollow Stables?"

"Max Regnery," Corey told him.

"He doesn't know anything about your school, does he?"

"No, I guess not," she answered.

"So, see, everybody's life has separate parts."

The pizza came. Corey took a slice and bit into it. As she chewed she thought about what her father had said.

"I guess so," she said a minute later. "But sometimes I wish I didn't have so many separate parts."

"Corey—your mother and I . . . ," her father began. Corey knew what her father was going to say. She'd heard it dozens of times and she knew it was true. That didn't mean she had to like it all the time.

"I know, Dad," she said. "You guys don't get along, but you each love me."

"Very much," Mr. Takamura added.

"But that's not what I was saying," Corey replied. "Sometimes I just wish I could be with May and Jasmine when I'm with you."

"We can do that," Mr. Takamura said.

"Would you like to invite them over to our apartment on your next visit?"

"Really?" Corey stared at her father.

"Sure," he told her. "It's your home. You can have your friends in it." He smiled. "Besides, I spent all of last weekend working on your bedroom. Wait till you see it. You're going to love it."

"I know," Corey said. And she meant it. She always loved home—both of her homes.

3 Samurai Goes for a Ride

"Meet you in our ring in ten minutes!" May said to Jasmine when they were getting off the school bus.

"Make it five!" Jasmine answered.

"Okay," May yelled, racing across her family's front lawn. It was Friday afternoon, the end of a long week of school and the beginning of a long weekend of pony riding. There wasn't a minute to waste.

May dropped her book bag on the floor of her room. She changed into her riding clothes and pulled on her boots. Her hard hat was in her closet. She kept it on a glob of papier-mâché that was originally supposed to be the head of an apatosaurus her second-grade class had made. It didn't look at all like the head of an apatosaurus. It looked a lot more like a glob of papier-mâché, but it worked perfectly as a hat rack.

May dashed downstairs. She couldn't wait to see Macaroni, but she wasn't in such a hurry that she forgot to pick up three carrots from the refrigerator.

One carrot was for Macaroni. The next was for Outlaw, just in case Jasmine forgot. And the third was for Samurai. May and Jasmine were planning to visit him. They could take Macaroni and Outlaw along, too. May was sure Samurai would like to have the ponies' company as well.

May loved walking into the stable in her backyard. Every time she did it, all the horses stuck their heads over their stall doors to greet her.

"Hello, Dobbin, Rascal, and Hank," she said, patting each one as she passed the stalls. Dobbin was her mother's horse. Her father rode Rascal, and Hank was the horse he used to ride. May's father said that Hank was semiretired. There was a new horse in the stable now, too. He was a big gray gelding named Double-O-Seven. He didn't belong to the Grovers.

Corey's Pony Is Missing

May's father trained horses for a living. His "students" sometimes stayed in the Grovers' stable so that Mr. Grover could work with them every day. Double-O-Seven was a good student. Mr. Grover thought that one day he'd be a champion jumper. Double-O-Seven was also a friendly horse. He nodded cheerfully when he saw May. She waved to him on her way to Macaroni's stall.

Macaroni pranced in his stall when he saw May. He knew what was coming. It was time for a ride!

"How are you?" May asked him.

He answered her by sniffing curiously at her pocket.

"You can smell a carrot from a mile away, can't you?" she asked. He opened his big brown eyes wide.

"You don't get a carrot by flirting with me," she told him. "You have to behave while I put your saddle on you."

Macaroni stood absolutely still while May put on his bridle and saddle. He even stood still while she tightened the girth on his saddle. That earned him his carrot.

He was still munching noisily when she led him out into the schooling ring. She was

19

about to climb into the saddle when Jasmine arrived, leading Outlaw. He was munching on a carrot, too.

"I brought a carrot for Macaroni," Jasmine said.

"And I've got one for Outlaw!" May told her.

Each girl gave the other's pony a treat. Then it was time for the best fun of all.

In just a few minutes, the girls were in their saddles and circling the ring together. They always walked their ponies first, to let them warm up. The ponies had to be properly warmed up before they trotted or cantered, or they might hurt their muscles. At the end of each ride, the girls had to walk them again, to let them cool down before they returned to their stalls.

May could feel Macaroni's stride becoming more comfortable as he walked around the ring. By the time he'd circled it three times, Macaroni was ready to go. So was Outlaw.

"Let's try those exercises Max told us about last week," May said. Jasmine nodded.

They began trotting in a pattern. First they circled the ring. Then they crossed through the center, changing directions. After that they made circles that got smaller and smaller

Corey's Pony Is Missing

and then changed directions and made circles that got larger and larger.

"I think I'm getting dizzy," May said.

"I think Outlaw's getting dizzy," Jasmine joked. "Let's go see Samurai now."

"Okay," May agreed.

The girls opened the gate to the schooling ring and rode to Samurai's stable.

Corey's house looked dark and empty. So did the stable. They tied their ponies to a post and went inside.

"Hello!" May called into the darkness. Samurai answered with a gentle snort.

"It looks like Samurai misses Corey, too," said May when they reached the pony's stall.

Jasmine looked at Samurai. She could see what May meant. The pony was standing in the back of his stall with his head down. His eyes looked dark and sad.

Jasmine opened the stall and walked in. Sam lifted his head and eyed her curiously. She gave him his carrot. He liked that. He sniffed her shirt pocket for another treat.

"Here," said May, pulling out the last carrot for Samurai. He liked that one, too.

They both agreed that he looked better now that he'd had a treat, but something was missing. He didn't have anyone to ride him.

Corey's Pony Is Missing

"Oh, yes, he does," May said suddenly. "He's got us!"

Jasmine knew exactly what she meant. Just because Corey wasn't there, Samurai didn't have to stay in his stall. The two members of the Pony Tails who were there could tack him up and ride him themselves!

Quick as could be, they fetched his tack and saddled him up. Then they took him back to the ring at May's house.

May walked Samurai around the ring two times while Jasmine rode Outlaw. Then Jasmine trotted on Samurai while May trotted on Macaroni. After that May took Samurai through all the exercises that Max had taught them. Finally Jasmine walked Samurai to cool him down.

"There, that's a good workout for you," Jasmine told the pony as she dismounted from the saddle.

Samurai took a deep breath and then blew out. It seemed like a sigh of contentment.

"Good job," said May. Corey hadn't asked them to exercise her pony, but May was glad they'd done it. That was part of taking care of their friend's pony while she was gone. Actually, it was a *big* part of taking care of Sam.

Now, though, it was getting late. It was time

23

to groom all three ponies and put them back in their stalls for the night.

They shared the work on Samurai. May gave his coat a brushing while Jasmine put his tack away. Then May brought him water and Jasmine put fresh hay in his manger. They both patted him. He went back into the corner of his stall.

"He looks lonely again," May said. "I wish there were something else we could do for him."

"We could open up the door to his yard," Jasmine suggested.

May wondered why she hadn't thought of that herself. Samurai's stall had a door in the back that opened onto a small yard. In good weather, Corey opened the yard door so that he could come and go as he pleased. Today was a nice day. Sam would probably love the fresh air.

Jasmine stepped into the stall and opened the door to the yard. Samurai sniffed at the breeze that came in. Then he stretched his neck out and peered into the yard.

"See, that brought him right out of the corner," said Jasmine, pleased with her idea.

"He looks much happier," May agreed.

"See you early tomorrow morning!" Jas-

Corey's Pony Is Missing

mine told Samurai as the two of them left, fastening the stall door securely behind them. They'd be bringing Sam to Pine Hollow tomorrow for their Pony Club meeting. Corey would be thrilled to see her pony, and he would be thrilled to see her.

May waved good-night to Jasmine and raced back to her own stable, ready to groom Macaroni and settle him down for the night. She had a good feeling inside. She and Jasmine had worked hard on their lessons, and they'd done something nice for Corey's pony. That was what being best friends meant, and the Pony Tails were definitely best friends!

4 Where Is Samurai?

The next morning, May got up bright and early. It was Saturday, the day of the Pony Club meeting. Today was a mounted meeting, which meant that the members would be riding at the meeting. Sometimes they had unmounted meetings, where they learned about such things as feeding and grooming horses. As far as May was concerned, mounted meetings were much better!

She hopped out of bed and got ready for the day. She put on her riding pants and boots and a warm shirt and jacket. Then she scooped up her hat from the apatosaurus's head.

After a hurried breakfast, she and her father went out to the stable to get Macaroni and load him, along with his tack and his grooming bucket, into the van. Macaroni was as good about getting into the van as he was about everything else. He walked right up the ramp and went straight into his little stall. May cross-tied him and closed the gate behind him.

Outlaw was another story. He didn't like getting into the van, so they had to play a trick on him to get him up the ramp. May held his lead rope. Jasmine walked backward in front of him, holding a carrot just out of his reach.

Outlaw loved carrots more than he hated vans. He sniffed the carrot and stepped forward. Jasmine stepped backward. Outlaw sniffed and reached for the carrot. Jasmine walked up the ramp. Outlaw walked up the ramp. Jasmine backed into the stall. Outlaw walked into the stall. Jasmine gave Outlaw the carrot while Mr. Grover closed the gate behind him. While Outlaw was still munching, May and Jasmine exited through the little doorway at the front of the stall. It was done.

Jasmine shook her head in wonder. "That trick works every time. Do you think it means Outlaw is dumb?"

"Nope," May told her. "I think it means he knows it's a good way to get a carrot!" They laughed about that as they went over to Corey's stable to get Samurai for the trip to Pine Hollow.

"Good morning!" May called cheerfully as she walked into the stable. She listened for a snort, but there was none. "Samurai?" she said. He still didn't answer. May hurried over to his stall. Jasmine was right behind her. But the stall was empty.

"Samurai? Where are you?" May stood on her tiptoes to see if he was lying in the hay by the door. He wasn't there.

"He must be in the yard," said Jasmine. The two girls entered the stall and walked through it to the yard. Samurai wasn't in the yard.

They looked in the corners; they looked behind the door. They even looked under the straw in the stall. There was no sign of Samurai.

May's stomach churned. "He's gone!" she shrieked.

"This is so terrible!" Jasmine said. "Where can he be?"

"What's the matter, girls?" Mr. Grover called as he poked his head inside the stable.

"We can't find Samurai!" May told him.

Mr. Grover frowned. "There's no time for

jokes. You're due at your meeting—with Samurai—in about half an hour.''

"It's not a joke, Dad," May said urgently. "Samurai isn't in his stall or in his yard."

It didn't take long for Mr. Grover to see that May was right.

"I can't believe this!" May wailed. "He must have been stolen!"

"Or he ran away!" said Jasmine.

"Maybe Corey came by earlier with her father and took him over to Pine Hollow herself," Mr. Grover suggested.

"Maybe," May said. But she sounded doubtful.

"That has to be the answer," Jasmine added. But inside she wasn't sure, either. In fact, she didn't believe it for one second.

When Mr. Grover pulled into Pine Hollow a short while later, Corey was standing in the driveway waiting for them. May's heart sank as Corey waved eagerly. It was the kind of wave a girl made when she was expecting to see her beloved pony in a few minutes. It wasn't the kind of wave a girl made when she already had her pony.

"Oh, no," said Jasmine. Corey had a lead rope in her hand. Corey thought she was go-

Corey's Pony Is Missing

ing to clip the rope to Samurai's halter and take him off the van.

"I can't look," May whispered.

Corey watched as her two best friends climbed out of Mr. Grover's car. They were getting out very slowly. May stared straight at the ground. Jasmine looked as though she had tears in her eyes. Something was wrong. Corey just knew it.

Corey dashed over to the back of the van hitched to the Grovers' car. She opened the door. It took only a second for her to see that there weren't three ponies back there. There were only two—and neither of them was Samurai.

She dropped the lead rope and turned to her friends. "You forgot my pony!"

Jasmine shook her head. "No, we didn't," she said softly. "We went to get him, but . . ." Tears streaked down her cheek.

"Oh, Corey!" May said. "Samurai is . . . *missing!*"

5 Comforting Corey

Corey was stunned. "What happened?" she asked.

Neither of her friends seemed to be able to tell her.

"We're not sure," Mr. Grover jumped in. "His stall was empty and he wasn't in his yard. The door to his stall was securely fastened, so he didn't get out that way, and there was no sign of damage to the fence in the yard."

"Someone stole him!" Corey cried.

"That's what I think," May chimed in.

"I don't think so, girls." Mr. Grover shook his head. "A horse thief is more likely to be interested in a champion like Double-O-Seven in our stable. Sam's a wonderful pony, but he's not all that valuable."

"But why would Sam run away?" Corey asked. "Why would he do that?"

Mr. Grover shrugged. "Maybe he wanted to explore his surroundings."

"But how could he get out?" wailed Corey. "Our yard is fenced in."

"He probably jumped," said Mr. Grover. He patted Corey's shoulder. "When Sam gets cold, hungry, and tired, he'll be jumping right back over that fence. I don't think you have anything to worry about."

"That's right," added May. She gave her friend a hug. "I bet he'll be home by this afternoon."

"Of course he will," Jasmine agreed. "He'll remember the delicious carrots he gets at home. Besides, where is there to go?"

Corey felt a little better. Mr. Grover and her friends seemed so sure that Samurai was okay. Corey had to believe them. Besides, as Jasmine said, where could Sam go?

But the more Corey thought about that, the worse she felt. Samurai could go a lot of places. Behind their houses there were dozens of fields connected to one another. And then there was the forest. It was hundreds of acres. It had steep trails, tricky hills, sharp rocks, deep water, and even a few cliffs. The woods were dangerous!

"Sam could be anywhere!" Corey cried suddenly. "I've got to go look for him!"

"Now, now, don't worry, Corey," Mr. Grover said again. "And don't start dreaming up awful things that could happen. I'm going home and I'll take Rascal out to look to see where Sam went."

"I'm coming with you!" said Corey.

"I think you should stay here," Mr. Grover replied.

"What if you don't find him?" Corey wailed.

"I'll find him," Mr. Grover said firmly. "And when I do I'll bring him right over to Pine Hollow."

"Promise?" she asked.

"I promise," he answered solemnly. "Now, in the meantime, Max'll have another pony you can ride. I want you to concentrate on Horse Wise and don't worry about Samurai. I'll take care of all the worrying on that."

Suddenly there was a flurry of activity in the stable behind them.

"Horse Wise, come to order!" Max called out.

Corey's Pony Is Missing

"Yipes!" said May. "The meeting's about to begin and we haven't even unloaded the ponies!"

Corey helped her friends get their ponies out of the van. She always liked to help, but this time it was especially important. The sooner the ponies were off the van, the sooner Mr. Grover could go back to her mother's house, and the sooner he'd return with Samurai. Today there was no time to waste.

6 Corey's Bad Day

Corey tried hard to concentrate at Horse Wise, but it wasn't easy—even when Max tried to help her. Max was the man who owned Pine Hollow. He gave most of the lessons, and he was in charge of Horse Wise. When it came to horses, Max was all business. The riders sometimes joked that he could see eight mistakes a rider was making all at the same time! Today Max knew that Corey needed special attention. He tried to help her.

"Why don't you ride Penny, Corey," he suggested after he heard what had happened.

Corey nodded and headed toward the pony's stall. Penny was a nice pony—a pretty, copper-colored mare with a sweet disposition. Normally Corey liked to be with her. But

Corey's Pony Is Missing

today, while she put on the pony's tack, she was listening for Mr. Grover's van in the Pine Hollow driveway.

"Corey, you forgot to put on Penny's bridle," Max said gently.

When Horse Wise lined up so that Max could inspect the horses' tack, she was listening for the phone to ring with good news.

"Corey, you're supposed to face me, not the fence," Max said.

When Max told the riders to warm up their horses, Corey was hoping Mrs. Reg would come in to say that Samurai had come home. Mrs. Reg was Max's mother. She was the stable manager.

"Corey, you should be walking Penny, not standing still," Max said.

And when it was time for them to begin their circling exercises, all she could think of was Samurai.

She saw him standing in his stall, peering over the door as she came toward him. She could almost feel his soft nose in her hand when she gave him a treat. She could smell his sweet pony smell when she gave him a hug. She could hear his soft nicker of pleasure while she groomed him and made his coat shine.

Pony Tails

"Corey, you should be circling in the other direction," Max called out.

She heard Max's words, but it was almost as if she couldn't understand them. Her mind was so full of thoughts about Samurai, there wasn't room for anything else. She thought about Samurai in his stall, Samurai in his yard, Samurai on a trail ride, Samurai in a schooling ring, and Samurai jumping.

He was a good jumper. He was a very good jumper. But was he a good enough jumper to go over the fence in his ring? Had he really done that by himself? And, if he had done it, why had he done it? Wasn't he happy?

Corey always tried to treat her pony well. But the more she thought about it, the more she realized she wasn't always good to Samurai. Once she'd forgotten to give him his breakfast until almost lunchtime. Sometimes she was in such a rush when she groomed him that she didn't do a very good job. Maybe he could tell that she really didn't like mucking out his stall. Maybe he'd run away to get away from her!

"Okay, everybody pair up and let's see you march down the center of the ring in a rising trot. Divide up at the far end, circling back. May, stay with Corey," said Max.

Corey's Pony Is Missing

Corey was only slightly aware of May riding next to her. May clucked her tongue, and Penny began to trot. Automatically Corey began posting, rising and sitting with Penny's gait as Max had instructed. She hardly noticed when they got to the end of the ring and she turned to the left. May circled to the right.

"Good job, Corey. Thanks, May," said Max. "This time, alternate pairs right and left," Max told the riders.

Samurai wasn't in his stable now. He wasn't in his yard. He wouldn't be looking over his stall the next time she walked in. She wouldn't be able to hug him or groom him, feed him, or bring him water. Worst of all, she wouldn't be able to ride him. She couldn't even muck out his stall. He was gone.

Corey gasped.

"It's okay, Corey," May said when they paired up again at the far end of the ring. "He'll come home. I *know* he will."

"But what if . . ." Corey couldn't even say it. All she could see in her mind was an empty stall and an empty yard. Her eyes filled with tears. She blinked, hoping nobody would notice.

"Good job," said Max. "I need to work with Stevie, Carole, Lisa, Veronica, Adam, and Meg for a while. The rest of you take a break for half an hour, okay?"

Corey dismounted and led Penny back to her stall. She remembered to loosen the pony's girth. She remembered to close and lock the stall door. She didn't think she could remember any more than that. All she could think about was Samurai. Now the tears started coming faster, and there wasn't anything she could do to stop them.

"Oh, Corey!" said Jasmine, running over to her friend. Jasmine gave Corey a hug. Corey hugged back. She needed her friends.

"He really *will* come home," May said as she joined them. "He's just curious about the world outside. Remember how he had to explore everything when you first moved in?"

Corey did remember, but that didn't stop her crying.

"And if he doesn't come home on his own," May continued, "Dad will find him. He knows everything about horses and ponies, remember?"

Corey shook her head. "But what if he can't find Sam? What if Sam ran away because he hates me?"

Watching her friend cry was more than Jas-

Corey's Pony Is Missing

mine could bear. "It's all my fault," she said. "We should never have let him into his yard yesterday!"

"What do you mean?" Corey demanded. She turned to look at her friend. "You let him into the yard? He should have been in his stall!"

"But—but—" Jasmine began.

"I mean—we just—" May tried.

"It's just that, well, he seemed so *lonely*," Jasmine added. "We wanted him to have something interesting to do. So we exercised him and left the door to his yard open."

"And you let him in the yard when the weather's nice, don't you?" May asked.

Corey swallowed hard. May was right. She *did* let Sam into the yard. He loved it out there. And her friends had only been trying to help. "I'm sorry," she said finally to May and Jasmine. "I didn't mean to yell at you. I'm just so upset. I would have let Sam out, too."

"I think Sam missed you, Corey," Jasmine said. "When you left for your father's, he watched your every step until you went into the house."

Corey closed her eyes. She could see Sam watching her. She could feel how lonely he was. And if he had been lonely in the stable without her, he must be much lonelier lost in the woods.

Then she felt bad all over again. She cried harder.

Corey's friends led her into Mrs. Reg's office to a box of tissues. Corey used the tissues, but she also wanted to use the phone.

"I can't stay here anymore. I have to go to my mom's and see for myself," she told her friends.

She called her father and told him what had happened. He said he was on his way. While May and Jasmine untacked Penny, Corey stood in the driveway at Pine Hollow, terrible thoughts filling her mind.

* * *

Corey and her father walked past the house and into Samurai's stable.

It was completely quiet inside. There was no sound of nickering or snorting and no gentle stomping or quiet munching. In the empty yard, the only motion was the soft shifting of the grass in the breeze.

No gates were unlocked. No rails were knocked down on the fence. The only thing amiss was that Samurai was gone.

Corey's Pony Is Missing

Corey had thought it would make her feel better to see the stable for herself. She was wrong. The empty stall only made her sadder.

"Oh, Daddy!" she said. "I can't believe he's gone!"

Her father picked her up and hugged her hard. "We'll find him, Corey. I promise. Mr. Grover will call us as soon as he has any news. In the meantime, staying here will just make you sadder. Let's go."

Corey buried her face in her father's shoulder.

"I found some new wallpaper for your room," he whispered softly. "It's got ponies on it. Would you like to help me put it up?"

Corey knew that her father was trying to make her feel better. Both of them knew it wouldn't work, though. There was only one thing that would make her feel better, and he was far, far away.

But she said okay and took her father's hand after he set her back down on the ground. Then they went back to his apartment.

7 May and Jasmine Get to Work

When Jasmine entered the Grovers' stable, May was cleaning Macaroni's stall. Mr. Grover was across the aisle, grooming Rascal.

"Did you see anything?" Jasmine asked Mr. Grover.

He shook his head sadly. "Not a thing," he said. "I looked in all the nearby fields. I followed all the main trails in the woods. I must have crossed the creek eight times. There was no sign of him on the hill or at the quarry. He's got to be out there somewhere, but I don't know where."

"Did you go by the rocky trail?" May asked.

"No, I didn't try that one," Mr. Grover said. "But I took the trail that runs right above it.

44

Corey's Pony Is Missing

I'm sure I would have seen or heard him if he'd been near the rocky trail."

"Were you calling for him?" Jasmine asked.

"Sure. I called his name, and a couple of times I watched for some sign from Rascal that there was another horse around. The woods were as quiet as can be. He wasn't there." Mr. Grover shrugged.

"But maybe you'll find him tomorrow," said May.

"I don't think there's any point in looking any more. I'm convinced he's going to come home on his own," said Mr. Grover. He gave Rascal's coat a final brush and then dropped the brush in his grooming bucket. "There's nothing to do now but wait," he said. "Trust me, girls. It's the best thing to do, even if it's tough."

"Dad!" May protested. "Are you just giving up?"

"No, not at all," Mr. Grover said. "Horses are hard to read sometimes. That's been true of Sam ever since he moved into the neighborhood. I have a feeling that Sam is still getting used to his new home. Maybe he needs to be by himself right now. When he needs to be back home, he'll come back home."

Pony Tails

"Do you really think so, Mr. Grover?" Jasmine asked.

"I really think so," Mr. Grover told her. He clicked the lock on Rascal's stall and stepped into the corridor.

As a trainer, Mr. Grover knew a lot about horses. May wanted to believe what he was saying—that Sam would return when he was ready—but it was hard to just sit around.

"Dad," May began, "if you're not going to go looking for him again tomorrow, is it okay if Jasmine and I go out on our ponies? We should go on the rocky trail—and the little one by the blueberry patch. You didn't go there. We should do it."

"But you don't know that part of the forest," he said.

"We know most of the trails," Jasmine said.

"No," he told them. "It's not a good idea at all. It's not safe for the two of you to wander there by yourselves."

"Come with us, then," May pleaded.

"I can't, May. Tomorrow's a busy day. I suppose we could try on Monday." He thought for a moment and then nodded. "I'll meet you girls here after school on Monday," he promised.

Corey's Pony Is Missing

Both girls watched him go back to the house. May looked at Jasmine. Jasmine looked at May. Waiting until Monday to look for Samurai felt like waiting forever.

"Come on, let's talk," May said. She closed the door on Macaroni's freshly cleaned stall and latched it securely. The two girls climbed the ladder that led to the hayloft in the Grovers' stable. It was the Pony Tails' favorite meeting place.

May sat on one bale of hay. Jasmine sat on another.

"We have to do something," said May.

"We already have," Jasmine reminded her. "If it weren't for us, Samurai would still be in his stall!"

"No way, Jasmine," said May. "It wasn't our fault. Corey leaves that door open, too. She told us that she probably would have let him out, just like we did."

"Maybe we did something else that Sam didn't like," said Jasmine.

"Oh, yeah, right, like exercising him, grooming him, and giving him carrots?" May shook her head. "We cheered him up and got him some exercise. That's all we did."

Jasmine had to admit that May had a point.

They *hadn't* done anything wrong. "But we still have to do something to get him back," she said.

"That's what I said," replied May.

The two girls sat in the loft, thinking. May had her elbows on her knees and her chin in her hands. She tapped her cheek with her right index finger. It didn't help her think.

Jasmine scrunched her lips together, making an awful face. It didn't help her think, either. They were both quiet for a while.

"We have to let people know Sam's missing. Just because we haven't seen him doesn't mean somebody else hasn't," said May.

"Maybe we should go knock on doors in the neighborhood," Jasmine suggested.

"Maybe—but if he were in the neighborhood, Dad would have found him this morning," May replied.

They thought some more.

"Maybe we should put an ad in the paper," Jasmine suggested.

"Great idea—but it doesn't come out until Thursday," said May.

"I've got it!" May announced. "It's a brainstorm!"

Jasmine sat up expectantly. "What?" she asked.

Corey's Pony Is Missing

"We can hire a helicopter to go over the woods and look for Samurai. You can see practically everything from a helicopter!"

Jasmine sighed. Sometimes May's brainstorms were more storm than brain. This seemed like one of those times.

"Like we could really hire a helicopter," Jasmine said.

"A balloon?" May suggested. Jasmine shook her head. "A blimp?"

"May!" Jasmine cried.

May put her chin back in her hands. "Someone's got to see him sooner or later," she said, "and that someone needs to know we're looking for him. How about we have the governor declare a state of emergency?" May wasn't exactly certain what a state of emergency was, but it sounded as if it would help Samurai.

"I don't think this is an emergency—"

"You would if it were your pony," May interrupted.

"Well, I don't think the *governor* will think it's a state of emergency," Jasmine replied.

"You're probably right," May said glumly. "He doesn't have his own pony. He probably wouldn't care at all." She put her chin back in her hands.

They thought some more.

Pony Tails

"Maybe we should—" Jasmine began.

"—put up signs!" May and Jasmine finished the sentence together.

"Jake!" they said. Then they gave each other a high five and a low five. That was what they always did when they said exactly the same thing at exactly the same time. They were such good friends that it often seemed as if they could read each other's mind.

"Let's use Mom's computer," May said, sliding down off her bale of hay. "That way we can make a hundred signs really fast."

A few minutes later, the two girls were at the keyboard of Mrs. Grover's computer.

"Write it big," said Jasmine.

May made the words as big as they could be and still fit on a piece of paper.

**Corey's Pony Is Missing!
Beautiful Bay Pony with
Sword-Shaped Blaze**

**Missing since Saturday
Morning
Call Corey at 555-5835
REWARD!!!!!**

Corey's Pony Is Missing

"Reward?" asked Jasmine, reading the words on the computer screen.

"Sure," said May. "That'll encourage people to look for him, not just wait for him to show up."

"But how are we going to pay a reward?" Jasmine asked, shaking her head. The last thing they needed right now was one of May's crazy ideas.

May stared at her friend for a second. She didn't want to admit it, but Jasmine had a good question. May had only $1.87. That wasn't much of a reward. "Maybe a reward doesn't have to be money," she said finally.

"Then what will it be?" asked Jasmine.

"A very nice thank-you. The person who finds Sam will be rewarded by knowing they've done the right thing," said May.

"May!" Jasmine exclaimed. "That's not enough."

"Maybe you're right," admitted May. "But I bet that the Takamuras would be willing to give a reward."

"Probably," Jasmine said, relenting. They left the poster the way May had typed it.

They printed 100 copies of the sign, borrowed tape from Mrs. Grover's desk, and headed out on their bicycles.

Pony Tails

They stopped at the first telephone pole they came to. May held the poster, and Jasmine taped it. They did the same at the next telephone pole, and every one after that. When they got into the shopping center near town, they asked the store owners if they could put them in the windows. Most of them said yes. A few said no.

"I'm never shopping there!" May declared, pointing to the store that had just refused her. "I'll just take my business elsewhere!"

"I should hope so," Jasmine said, giggling. "That was a liquor store!"

May's eyes opened wide. She'd been concentrating so hard on what she was asking, she hadn't even noticed *where* she was asking. "Whoops," she said. "Well, when I grow up—if I ever get to be *that* old—I'm still taking my business elsewhere!"

"Let's try the newspaper store next," said Jasmine. A few minutes later, there was a sign in the newsstand's window. There was also one in the drugstore, the jewelry store, the shoe store, the music store, and the crafts shop. The coffee shop put one on the bulletin board. The ice cream shop, named Tastee Delight and always called TD's for short, put one on the door.

Pony Tails

"Want to take a break?" Jasmine asked May. "My treat," she added, remembering May had only $1.87.

That sounded like a really good idea. They parked their bikes outside TD's and went in for a treat. They sat at the counter. Jasmine ordered a dish of vanilla ice cream with sprinkles. May wanted a root beer float. She put the remaining posters on the counter beside her. There were only a few left. They'd done a lot of work in a short time. Worrying about Samurai's being alone someplace had made Jasmine and May move fast.

"Do you suppose he's hungry?" May asked.

Jasmine didn't have to ask who "he" was. She knew May was talking about Samurai.

"I bet he's found some sweet grass to munch on," said Jasmine.

"Maybe you're right, but I hope he hasn't hurt himself," said May. "What if he fell or tripped on something?"

"Why do you always have to think of awful things? Maybe somebody's already taking care of him," said Jasmine. "Anyone who found him would be sure to love him and look after him."

"*If* they found him," said May. "He could be

Corey's Pony Is Missing

deep in the woods where hardly anyone goes."

"We go there," Jasmine said. "We ride all over some parts of the woods all the time. If he's there *we* would find him."

"But we're here," said May. "We're not out there looking for him when awful things could be happening to him."

"But what we're doing here is important," said Jasmine. "And besides, do you think our parents would let us ride in that part of the woods together—just the two of us?"

Jasmine had a point. Their parents usually didn't like it when only two of them were riding in the woods, especially on the rocky trail. A bigger group was a safer group. And Mr. Grover had specifically said they couldn't go. Jasmine's parents would say exactly the same thing.

The waitress brought their orders. She saw the posters on the counter.

"A lost pony?" she asked. "I hope you get him back before anything happens to him."

May and Jasmine exchanged looks. The waitress had said exactly what was on both of their minds. Placing blame or worrying wasn't important. Finding Samurai was.

Pony Tails

"We *have* to go look ourselves," said May. "No matter what Dad said."

Jasmine nodded. "I know. But it's too late to go today. Look, it's dark out already."

"First thing in the morning," May vowed. "We'll leave before the sun is up. Maybe they'll never even notice!"

8 Hunting for Samurai

Jasmine was up and out of bed before the sun came up on Sunday morning. She was dressed in her riding clothes and downstairs five minutes after that. She almost made it out of the house without her mother's knowing it. But when she realized she had forgotten her hard hat, she had to go back upstairs. Her mother heard the thunk of her boots on the stairs.

"Where are you going at this hour?" Mrs. James asked, opening the door to her bedroom.

Jasmine gulped. "May and I are riding out on the rocky trail to look for Samurai."

"Alone?" Mrs. James asked.

"With each other," Jasmine said. She hoped that sounded like a lot of people.

"Jasmine, the rocky trail can be dangerous. You can't go riding there with just May," said Mrs. James.

"You've let us go on picnics in the woods," Jasmine reminded her.

"I knew exactly where you were going then and it was the middle of summer, not this cool weather," her mother said.

"Mom, this is an emergency!" Jasmine said. "Our best friend's pony is missing, and it's partly our fault. We just have to do *something.*"

Mrs. James looked at Jasmine. Her frown softened. "Promise me you'll be careful," her mother said.

"We always are," Jasmine told her.

"Good luck," said her mother. Jasmine gave her a hug. That was to thank her for understanding how important it was to go looking for Samurai.

It took her only a few minutes to tack up Outlaw and lead him over to May's stable. Jasmine greeted Rascal, Dobbin, Hank, and Double-O-Seven. The horses peered curiously over the doors of their stalls in the dim light of the dawn.

Corey's Pony Is Missing

"We've got to find Samurai," she explained to them. "That's why I'm here so early."

Jasmine's words seemed to satisfy their curiosity. They pulled their heads back into their own stalls. Jasmine could hear the idle munch of hay behind her as she proceeded to Macaroni's stall.

May's pony greeted her with a curious look. He whinnied a friendly hello at Outlaw. Outlaw whinnied back. Jasmine was about to explain their mission to Macaroni when May dashed into the stable. She had run all the way from her house. She was carrying a backpack, and she had a granola bar in her hand.

"Mom caught me sneaking out of the house. I was afraid she'd stop me. But all she said was I had to have breakfast." May pointed to the granola bar. "She also said I had to take snacks and drinks for you and me. That's what's in the backpack. I guess she understands."

"My mom, too," said Jasmine. "Only she didn't give me a granola bar—just a warning to be careful."

"Here, help yourself," May said. She opened the backpack to reveal a dozen granola bars and four juice boxes.

59

Jasmine took a bar and ate it while May tacked up Macaroni. "We could survive for weeks on all this food." Jasmine smiled.

May shrugged. "It could take us a while to find Sam."

Jasmine nodded. She didn't want to think about it, but May was right. Who knew how far Corey's pony had strayed?

The girls checked each other's tack to be sure everything was in order. Outlaw's girth needed to be tightened a notch. May helped Jasmine do it. May had gotten Macaroni's reins tangled. Jasmine helped her straighten them out. Then they were ready to leave.

Behind the schooling ring at May's house was a large field that belonged to the Grovers. On the other side of the field were woods that belonged to the state. The woods were filled with trails for horses, hikers, and cyclists. On the other side of the forest were more fields and Pine Hollow Stables.

"It's possible that Samurai went out and found a horse or a cow in a field to be his friend," said Jasmine. "Maybe we should circle around the woods and look at the fields."

"If that's the case, then he's not really in trouble and someone will find him. I think we'd better look where he could be in trouble," said May.

That sounded scary to Jasmine, but it made sense. May went first, following a trail they knew. It was a curvy trail that snaked up a hill.

The sun was fully up now. It was going to be a bright, clear day. Normally it was the kind of day the Pony Tails liked best for riding.

Around them the woods were cool and fresh and inviting. The leaves were starting to turn, so there were patches of red, orange, and yellow among the green. In such a nice place, it was hard to think of bad things. Jasmine found herself feeling more and more confident that Samurai was safe and that they would find him.

"I bet Samurai found sweet grass to eat," said Jasmine.

"What if it's a weed that makes him sick?" asked May. "Horses and ponies often have trouble when their feed is changed."

"He probably found fresh water to drink," said Jasmine. "That would be good for him."

"It could be, but some of the water in the woods isn't too clean. Remember the pond that has all the green stuff in it?" May asked. "That wouldn't be good for him at all."

Of course May was right. The green water would be no better than the bad weeds. "But don't you think he'd enjoy walking through these pretty woods?" Jasmine asked.

"As long as he didn't trip on something or get a stone in his shoe or wander so far that we'll never find him," said May.

Jasmine wasn't feeling as good anymore. Every time she thought of something nice that could be happening to Samurai, May thought of something awful!

"Oh, gosh, I hope he's okay," said Jasmine.

"Me too," said May.

They rode the trail to the top of the hill. There was a lot of grass along the trail for a pony to eat, but there was no sign of Samurai. They came back down the hill along another trail. It followed the small brook that turned into Willow Creek. There was plenty of cool, clean water for a pony to drink along that trail. But Samurai wasn't there.

They rode through a glade where a pony could find shelter in case it rained. They didn't find Samurai there, either. They followed a path to the old rock quarry. A pony could get into a lot of trouble there. He could slip or trip or get stuck in mud by the pond. They didn't see Samurai there, either.

They stopped in a clearing in the woods to have a snack. The girls loosened the reins and let their ponies graze idly on the grass that grew there. It seemed fair for the ponies to snack when the riders snacked. May unzipped the backpack. She handed Jasmine a granola bar and some apple juice. Jasmine looped her reins around her wrist and punched the straw through the top of the juice box. She was concentrating on her snack and didn't see Outlaw's ears flicking anxiously.

She noticed that something was wrong when he lifted his head and began a nervous dance.

"Calm down, Outlaw," she said. She reached forward to pat his neck. That usually reassured him. This time it didn't. He whinnied and stomped. Jasmine reached to tighten up on the reins. She found that she had a granola bar in one hand and a juice box in the other hand. She didn't have the reins in any hand at all. The reins had dropped loosely on Outlaw's neck.

There was a sudden gust of cool wind. That

was all it took to set Outlaw off altogether. First he bucked, and then he ran.

Jasmine had totally lost control. When Outlaw bucked, she slid out of the saddle onto the ground and landed on her bottom. She found herself sitting there, completely unharmed, with a granola bar in one hand and a juice box in the other. She was helpless to do anything but watch her pony run away.

Luckily Outlaw didn't run very far. He went only to the other side of the glade. Then he stopped and turned around and looked at Jasmine. His ears weren't flicking anymore. His feet weren't dancing. He didn't look nervous or frightened. He just looked surprised. That was how Jasmine felt, too.

"Naughty pony!" she said. "You are a very naughty boy!"

He stepped toward her. She stood up.

"I'll get him," May offered.

"No, I think he'll come here," said Jasmine. She was right. Outlaw hung his head in shame and kept his eyes on the ground, but he walked right back to Jasmine. "He knows he shouldn't have done that," Jasmine said.

"He looks the way I did when my mother found out I'd erased a whole file from her computer," May said. "I really didn't mean to

cause trouble, but I sure managed to do it and I knew it. So did my mother."

"Outlaw didn't mean to do it, either," said Jasmine. "Sometimes he just can't keep himself from being naughty, though."

"I wonder why," May said thoughtfully.

"Who knows?" asked Jasmine, taking Outlaw's reins. She patted him and then remounted. He didn't take a step. He behaved perfectly. "It's just the way he is."

Nothing was broken; nobody was hurt. It was time to get going.

The girls followed the trails in the woods for another hour. They found a group of hikers. None of them had seen a pony on the loose. Then the girls met up with a group of riders from Pine Hollow. They hadn't seen Samurai. May and Jasmine even stopped some boys on dirt bikes to ask them if they'd seen Samurai. They hadn't.

Jasmine found herself feeling very sad about Samurai. She'd hoped for at least a small sign that he had been around, but there was nothing. Her mood didn't improve when May said it was time for them to get back home. Their ponies had had enough of a ride for one day.

Corey's Pony Is Missing

"What if we never find him?" Jasmine asked.

"Of course we'll find him," May said. "Remember how Outlaw returned to you when he ran away? Well, Samurai will do the same thing."

9 Corey Comes Home

When she woke up Sunday morning, Corey blinked twice. She couldn't remember where she was. The wallpaper in her bedroom was covered with ponies. It took a moment to remember that this was the new wallpaper in her bedroom at her father's apartment. She smiled at all the ponies. She blinked again. Then she remembered that Mr. Grover had called yesterday to say he hadn't found her pony. Samurai was still missing. She stopped smiling.

"Good morning, sugar," Mr. Takamura said, peering into her room. "I've got some pancake batter ready and the bacon is all done. Are you ready for your favorite breakfast?"

Corey's Pony Is Missing

Corey wasn't ready for breakfast. She didn't have any appetite at all. She hadn't had any appetite for Pat's pizza yesterday. She couldn't be hungry when all she could think of was Samurai wandering somewhere alone.

"I guess so," she said to her father. He was trying hard to cheer her up. She didn't want to hurt his feelings. She got out of bed and got dressed. She joined her father in the kitchen.

He was pouring batter onto the griddle when she came in. She sat at the table and watched him.

"I finished grading all my papers yesterday morning," he said. "That means I have the whole day off to spend with you. Is there something special you'd like to do?"

"Dad, I—I—" Corey stammered. She tried to smile for her dad, but she couldn't. She felt the tears welling in her eyes.

Her father hugged her. "It's Samurai, isn't it?"

She nodded, feeling the comfortable softness of his shirt on her cheek. "All I can think about is him. I'm so worried."

"Why don't you call your friends?" Mr. Takamura suggested. "Maybe Sam showed up this morning."

Corey thought that was a good idea. First

69

she called May. May wasn't in. Neither were May's parents. Corey asked May's sister, Ellie, where May was.

"Oh, she's off playing some sort of game or something on that pony of hers," Ellie said. Ellie didn't think much of her sister's pony.

Corey thanked her and hung up. Her mind filled with the image of May on Macaroni, having fun. Maybe they were practicing the exercises Max had given them. Maybe they were working on the jumps in the schooling ring. Whatever they were doing, Corey felt terribly lonely because she and Samurai weren't doing it, too.

She called Jasmine. There was no answer. Corey didn't want to leave a message. She was too miserable to say anything to a machine. She hung up the phone and stared at it.

After a while she decided to call her mother's house. Doc Tock's assistant, Jack, was there. He told Corey he'd be there all day looking after a dog that was very sick. Corey asked him about Sam.

"No," he said. "No, there's no sign of Samurai. I left the gate open to be sure he could get into his yard. I even put some fresh hay and feed out for him. He's not there. I'll call you the minute he gets here, though."

Corey's Pony Is Missing

That will be nice, Corey thought. But it would be even nicer to be there when Sam showed up. Suddenly Corey knew what she had to do.

"Dad, I have to go back to Mom's," Corey said.

Her father nodded. "I'm not surprised you feel that way," he said. "I'll drive you over and stay with you there until your mother gets home tonight."

"I know you wanted to do something special today," Corey apologized.

"We'll have other times to do something special together," Mr. Takamura said. "Right now, the most special thing that could happen would be for Samurai to come home. Let's go —okay?"

"Okay," she said.

It took her only a few minutes to eat some pancakes and then pack her bag. Not long after that, they were walking up the path to her mother's front door. Corey pushed open the door.

"Jack?"

"Hi, Corey," he said. He came into the hall from Doc Tock's clinic. He had a parrot on one shoulder and was holding a kitten in his hands. "No sign of him yet," he said. It was typical of Jack to understand that Corey had come home early because of a pet.

Corey thanked him. She left her suitcase in the front hall and went out into the backyard to Samurai's stable. Her father went to sit in the kitchen.

Sunshine came cheerfully through the slats of the stable. Corey could see hay dust in the streams of light. She could smell the sweet scent of clean hay. A fresh breeze brushed her hair. The stable was a nice place to be, except for one thing. It was silent. There was no welcoming whinny, no eager stomp of hooves. She could hear no contented chomping of a well-fed pony. Samurai was gone.

Corey slipped into the empty stall and looked at the bare straw that lined the floor. The gateway outside led to an empty yard.

Corey sat down in a corner of the stall and hugged her knees. She thought about Samurai. She thought about all the wonderful times they'd had together. She didn't know if she would ever ride him again, ever feed him again, or ever jump him again. And then her tears came. She cried silently. Her tears fell, one by one, onto the straw beneath her knees.

And when her last tear had fallen, there was still silence.

Corey's Pony Is Missing

Then Corey heard something. She almost felt the sound before she heard it. Something was thumping on the ground outside. Then it was stronger. It was definitely a pony's hooves. No, it was two ponies' hooves.

May and Jasmine were here! If she couldn't have her pony, at least Corey could have her friends. She went into Samurai's yard to greet them.

"Come on, Corey," May said from the yard where she was sitting on Macaroni. "Let's go over to my hayloft. At a time like this, the Pony Tails have to stay together."

Corey couldn't agree more. She hurried after her friends.

10 The Pony Tails Meeting

"And we put posters on every single telephone pole in all of Willow Creek," Jasmine said.

"A hundred of them?" Corey asked. She couldn't believe all the work her friends had done for her.

"Well, almost a hundred of them," May said. "We also asked the stores at the shopping center to put them up. They all did—except for the liquor store. That doesn't matter. People who buy liquor probably aren't thinking about ponies."

"Probably not," Corey agreed.

"But we called the places that *do* care about ponies," said Jasmine. "We called the animal shelters, the stables, the 4-H, and the nearby

Corey's Pony Is Missing

Pony Clubs, including Cross County. Everybody said they'd be on the lookout for Samurai."

"He's somewhere near," said May. "He just has to be. And if he is, someone will find him and call."

Corey blinked in disbelief. Was it only yesterday that she'd actually accused her best friends of carelessness? Now she couldn't believe how much love and care they were showing. She was ashamed all over again. She didn't know how to tell them how much it meant to her. "Thanks so much for everything you guys have done for me and Samurai," she said.

"But it hasn't worked yet," said Jasmine.

"It will," May said. "It will. And until he comes home, we'll go for a ride in the woods every single day."

The phone in the stable rang. May scooted down the ladder to answer it. It was Corey's mother, home early from New Orleans. It was time for the Pony Tails' meeting to end.

The girls promised to meet after school the next day with Mr. Grover to look for Samurai.

75

11 The Samurai Hunt

On Monday when Corey got home from school, there were three phone messages on the answering machine for her. Her heart raced as she listened to the messages.

"I'm calling about the missing pony . . ."

"I saw that poster . . ."

"We have a pony here that might be of interest to you . . ."

Corey called each person back right away. She was so nervous that her hand was shaking as she held the phone.

The first person she reached said she'd definitely seen a pony over the weekend. Was it Samurai? Corey wondered. She asked the woman to describe the pony she'd seen. "It was white with black patches," she said.

Corey's Pony Is Missing

Corey didn't know what pony that was, but it definitely wasn't Samurai. She thanked the woman for calling.

The second person was a girl who had a pony, too. She was calling to tell Corey how sorry she was that Samurai was missing. Corey thanked her, too, though she wasn't feeling very grateful. She was only feeling disappointed. But she still had one call to return. Maybe this would be the one.

"Hello—you called about my missing pony?" Corey said to the man who answered the phone.

"Oh, yes," he said. "Thanks for calling me back. Listen, I have a pony here—"

"A dark bay with a crescent-shaped blaze?" Corey asked eagerly.

"Oh, no. This one's a gray. He's a real nice pony, gentle as can be. He's been ridden by a lot of kids and he's a fine pony, I can assure you. Since you're going to need a new pony . . ."

Corey couldn't believe it. This man wanted to sell her another pony! She didn't thank him. Instead she told him she wasn't interested and slammed down the phone.

How could three phone calls be so useless! And so disappointing, Corey thought with a sigh. Samurai, where are you? she wondered for the hundredth time since he'd disappeared.

Corey pulled on her jacket and hurried over to May's stable. She was supposed to meet May, Jasmine, and Mr. Grover there so that they could all go out and search the woods again.

Mr. Grover was in the schooling ring setting up jumps for his student, Double-O-Seven. "Hi, Corey," he called. "Any sign of Sam yet?" She shook her head. "That's too bad," May's father went on. "I was hoping to help you girls search the forest this afternoon, but it looks like I'll have to stay here. Double-O-Seven's owner is due any minute. He wants to take a look at his horse's progress."

"That's okay, Mr. Grover," Corey replied. "Maybe the three of us will get lucky this afternoon. Sam has to be out there somewhere."

"C'mon, Corey," May called as she walked out of the Grovers' stable and mounted Macaroni. "Let's get going before it gets dark."

Corey hurried over to her friend and climbed on Macaroni's back behind May. The

Corey's Pony Is Missing

gentle pony didn't seem to mind the second passenger at all. In fact, Corey thought, it's as if he knows that we're going to search for his friend Samurai.

By four o'clock the girls were on the trail. By five o'clock they'd covered the hill, the stream, the quarry, and the glades. There was no sign of Samurai, and it was beginning to get dark.

They returned home, untacked their horses, and promised to go out again the next day. Corey's parents had decided to let Corey stay at her mother's house for the week, just in case Samurai showed up. On Saturday she would go to her father's after her Pony Club meeting. That gave her five long days to look for and to worry about Samurai. She and her friends made the best of the time, but the rest of the week was no better than Monday.

On Tuesday Corey had one phone message. She called back.

"I remember seeing Samurai," a girl named Elspeth said.

Corey's heart quickened.

"I came to Horse Wise once. You were there, with Samurai."

Corey's Pony Is Missing

"Yes?" said Corey. She was trying to remember who Elspeth was.

"He's a really nice pony," Elspeth told her. "I just want you to know that I'm sorry he's missing."

"Thank you," said Corey, though she didn't mean it. She remembered Elspeth now, and she knew she was just trying to be nice, but it wasn't helpful. The only thing that would help was information about where Samurai was!

"Good luck," said Elspeth.

Again the girls rode on the trails in the woods. This time Corey rode with Jasmine on Outlaw. Again they found nothing.

Every day Corey ran from the bus to the telephone answering machine to see if anyone had called. There were four more phone messages about the posters that May and Jasmine had put up. Two of them were from people who thought they'd seen ponies that might be Samurai, but when they described them, Corey knew neither was Sam. One was another call about the white-and-black pony. The other call was a total mistake.

"Oh, he's a pretty little fellow," said one man. "He has long spindly legs and a tiny little tail. He was standing in a field with a much bigger horse," he said.

81

Pony Tails

The man wasn't describing a pony, he was describing a newborn horse—a foal. The much bigger horse was the foal's mother. Corey could have explained that to the man, but she didn't bother. A lot of people thought ponies were just baby horses. Still, she thanked the man for calling.

"You're welcome," he said. "Just trying to help."

Corey told her friends about the calls. "And two more people who have a pony they want to sell have called me!" she said.

"People can be dumb," May remarked.

"It seems like they want to take advantage of you when you're sad," Jasmine remarked.

"Oh, I don't know," said Corey. "Mostly they just sound like they want to find a good home for a nice pony."

The girls kept looking, making calls to nearby animal shelters, farm associations, horse farms, and student groups. Nobody had seen Samurai. Nobody knew where he might be.

On Thursday the local newspaper came out. Corey's father had put an ad in it but so far no one had answered.

"Maybe people will call about the ad over

the weekend," Jasmine said as the three girls sat in the hayloft after their trail ride.

"I'll be at Dad's after Horse Wise on Saturday," Corey said.

"We can check for messages," May offered.

"Thanks, but Mom will be home," Corey told her. "She'll call me. You can do something much more important."

"Whatever it is, we'll do it," said Jasmine. "No matter how hard."

"I know," said Corey. "But this isn't hard. What you can do for me is to be with me. Will you come to my father's with me for a sleepover?"

"At your dad's apartment?" May asked.

"On Shelley Lane?" said Jasmine.

Corey nodded.

"Of course," May told her.

"Sure," added Jasmine.

"Good," said Corey. "Because my dad wants to meet my two best friends."

The phone in the stable rang once. That was Mrs. Grover's signal that dinner was almost ready. It was time for the girls to go home.

May waved good-bye to her friends and went to the house. She was thinking about Corey's father's apartment. She wondered what it would look like. She thought it would be odd to have a sleepover at a friend's house that wasn't her friend's house. Still, she'd be with her friends and she'd be helping Corey. That was what was important.

12 Reunion

Corey sat down on her bed and looked around her room. She was packing to go to her father's after Horse Wise. He'd pick her up there and take her and her friends to his apartment.

So much had changed in nine days. One of the things that had changed was that there was a new picture on her bedroom wall. It was a painting of a horse-drawn cab that her mother had brought Corey from New Orleans. It made Corey smile because the horse was wearing a straw hat with his ears sticking through it. It was a nice present. But having a painting of a horse wasn't the same as having Samurai.

Corey took a deep breath and sighed. She'd

ridden every inch of the woods. She'd looked in every corner of the fields near her home. She'd talked to a lot of strange people. And she'd cried. None of that had done any good at all.

Now she had another Horse Wise meeting, and it was a mounted meeting again so that they could practice their drills. Today Cross County, a nearby Pony Club, was going to have a joint meeting with them at Pine Hollow.

Corey could ride Penny. Penny was a nice pony. It wasn't her fault that she wasn't Samurai.

"Stop it," Corey told herself. Being glum wouldn't change anything. She decided to make the best of the situation. That reminded her that Jasmine and May could use her help to get their ponies into the van—especially Outlaw. He could be so naughty sometimes.

She finished dressing and packing and went downstairs. She gave her mother an extra hug and then went out the back door of her house, heading for May's.

She could hear the ruckus even before she got there.

"Come on, Macaroni. It's time to get in the trailer," May was saying.

Corey's Pony Is Missing

Macaroni whinnied.

"I think he's learned a few things from Outlaw," Jasmine said. "Outlaw is the one who's supposed to be fussy!"

"What's the problem?" Corey asked as she put her suitcase on the backseat of Mr. Grover's car. "Why is Macaroni fussing?"

"Beats me," said May. "Here, take a carrot, Corey. See if you can get him to do what he's supposed to do."

Corey took the carrot and began backing into the trailer, the way she and her friends usually did to trick Outlaw into getting in.

Macaroni sniffed toward the carrot. Corey backed up. Macaroni stood still.

"He's seen us do this to Outlaw. He doesn't want us to fool him!" said May. "Let me try something else."

The something else was a trick her father had shown her. She walked Macaroni away from the van. She walked him in circles three times around the van, totally ignoring the ramp. Then, the fourth time, she took a quick turn and led him up the ramp. He was in his stall before he knew what had happened. Corey clipped the stall door shut. May came out smiling.

"No trouble at all," she said.

"Keep the carrot handy. Here comes Out-law," said Jasmine.

Outlaw walked right up the ramp without a second of protest.

"I'm beginning to think there's no way of ever knowing what goes on in a pony's mind," Jasmine declared.

May clunked the trailer door shut and locked it. "I guess one thing we can count on with ponies is that they're never predictable," she said. She brushed her hands off and went back to her house to pick up her overnight bag.

Corey and Jasmine went to open the back doors of the station wagon. Behind it the trailer rocked ever so slightly. It was unusual for the ponies to fuss once they were inside. But these two ponies were clearly fussing.

"I think they're trying to tell us something," said Jasmine.

"They're trying to tell us it's time to get to Horse Wise," Corey said.

Inside the van one of the ponies whinnied.

Outside the van there was a whinnying answer.

May glanced toward her family's stable as she came back with her bag. "Double-O-

Corey's Pony Is Missing

Seven must have been chatting with Macaroni," she said. "Maybe they just want to finish their conversation."

Then another whinny came from the van, followed by another answer. But this time it didn't sound as if it was coming from the Grovers' stable.

The Pony Tails looked at one another. Could it be? They didn't even utter the words. They just ran.

Corey didn't dare hope, but she couldn't stop herself. The whinnying came again. Then Corey knew. She knew the whinny. She knew the voice. And she knew it was true.

Samurai was home!

There he was. He was standing impatiently outside his yard, stomping on the ground. He almost looked as if he were knocking on the door to get in. The minute he spotted Corey, he began nodding. She thought she could hear what he was thinking. *Yes, all right. Now you know it's me. It's about time you opened this gate and let me in. Do you think I'm going to wait all day?*

Corey ran faster than she could ever remember running.

"Samurai!" she cried as she reached him.

She flung her arms around his neck and hugged him tightly, rubbing her face in his soft, warm coat.

Can't you tell when a fellow needs a good dose of sweet feed?

Doc Tock came out the back door of her house. "What's all the— Samurai! You've come home!" she said.

May, Jasmine, and Doc Tock joined Corey in patting Samurai and welcoming him back.

"Is he okay, Mom? Is he?" Corey asked, stepping back to look at her pony.

Doc Tock took a look. "Seems to be," she said. "But let's be sure."

She ran her hands along his back and his legs, checking for problems. Then she looked at his eyes and his ears. She used her stethoscope to check his heart and lungs while Corey looked at his hooves.

"He's fine," Doc Tock announced. "I think he could use a good grooming and a square meal, but wherever he's been, it doesn't seem to have done him any harm."

Corey clipped a lead rope onto Samurai's halter and brought him back inside his stable. May and Jasmine closed the gate behind him and then shut the door to his yard.

"I guess you're going to want to keep him

securely cooped up for a long time now, aren't you?" May asked.

"No way," said Corey. "The thing I most want to do right now is to take him to Horse Wise. Can I, Mom?"

Doc Tock shrugged. "Don't know why not," she said. "But I think you'd better groom him and feed him and give him some water first. Do you think you know anyone who could help you with that?"

Corey didn't have to ask for help. Her two best friends volunteered instantly.

May and Jasmine were finishing up the last bit of work with a currycomb when they heard the honk of the Grovers' car. Mr. Grover didn't honk anymore when he saw what was keeping them.

He came and pitched in, too. He carried Samurai's tack to the van and then helped lead Samurai up the ramp. He closed and locked the door.

"Let's go!" he said.

The girls piled into the backseat. Later Corey couldn't remember anything that had happened or been said during the whole trip to Pine Hollow that day. All she could remember was that she'd never felt happier or more relieved in her whole life.

13 Corey's Other Home

"You can have the lights on for another half hour and then it's definitely lights out," said Mr. Takamura.

"Okay," said May agreeably. She liked Mr. Takamura a lot, so she wanted to sound agreeable. What she wasn't saying, though, was that the Pony Tails had long ago discovered that they could talk *after* lights were out.

May was surprised by how much she liked Mr. Takamura. Before they'd met him and been to his apartment, she and Jasmine hadn't been able to imagine what Corey's "other" life was like. Now they knew. Mr. Takamura had a pleasant apartment with a big kitchen, two bedrooms, and a nice living

93

room. Corey's room had twin beds. Mr. Takamura had brought in a folding cot so that each of the girls had a bed to sleep on.

"Your dad's apartment is a great place," said May.

"It's not just my dad's apartment," Corey said patiently. "It's my apartment, too. Just like my mother's house is my house, too."

May hadn't thought of it that way. But it made sense. Corey's parents each had one home, but Corey had *two* homes.

"Speaking of my mother, I think I'll call her again, just to be sure Samurai's all right."

May and Jasmine looked at each other and smiled when Corey went into the living room to make the call. This was the third time Corey had called her mother. Samurai had been just fine the two earlier times. They were pretty sure he would be fine this time, too.

Corey returned a few minutes later. "He's okay," she reported. "Mom's got him in his stall with the door closed to the yard. She called a carpenter this afternoon and he'll come next week to make the fence higher so Samurai can't run away again. Until then, we'll keep him inside."

Corey picked up her hairbrush and comb.

Corey's Pony Is Missing

She brushed her hair back and up, trying to make it into a ponytail like the ones her friends had. When she was done, she had a little tuft of hair in her hand.

"Almost?" she asked.

"Not yet," May said.

Corey sighed. She knew May was right. It was going to be a long time before she had a real ponytail. She could wait. It would be easier than waiting for Samurai to come home.

"Pass me a graham cracker, will you?" Jasmine asked.

May offered her the plate and took a cracker herself.

"So, how do you think we did today at Horse Wise?" Jasmine asked.

"Samurai and I had a wonderful time," Corey said, abandoning her hairbrush. "I don't know about you guys!"

May and Jasmine laughed. For two hours, Max had all the riders from Horse Wise and Cross County working on a drill exercise. It was hard work and took a lot of concentration. Corey and Samurai hadn't made one mistake.

"I think Samurai was as happy to be back

Corey's Pony Is Missing

home with me as I was to have him home," said Corey.

"Definitely," May agreed. "And you know what? I think Macaroni and Outlaw were glad to have him, too."

"I was thinking the same thing," said Jasmine. "Remember how funny they both were about getting in the van? I think they knew Sam was back home and that's why they were acting strange."

"Don't be silly," said Corey. "Ponies can't talk." She tossed a pillow at Jasmine as if to emphasize her point.

"Then why was Macaroni being so fussy while Outlaw was so gentle?" Jasmine asked, catching the pillow. "They were trying to tell us something."

Corey thought for a moment, then finally nodded. "I think you guys might be right. I only wish Samurai would tell me where he went."

"Too bad, because he won't," said May.

Her friends looked at her.

"There are some things that ponies can tell us," May went on, "like when they're happy or lonely. But I think it's right that horses and ponies have secrets. We're not supposed to know everything they think and do. They need to have their own lives, just like we have a life away from them."

"But I want to be with Sam all the time," Corey burst out. "I always want to be with our ponies."

"Well, would you really want to have three ponies in the room with us here, now?" May asked.

Corey and Jasmine laughed out loud.

"May," Jasmine groaned, "you have a funny way of making a point, but I guess I know what you mean."

"Me too," Corey added. "Besides, the ponies on the wallpaper are the only horses my dad allows in here!"

"You know," Corey said a moment later, when the laughter died down, "it makes Samurai seem mysterious. It's like he's got a secret life and I'll never know what it is."

"Just like the way May and I thought *you* had a secret life, here in your father's apartment," said Jasmine.

"And like the secret life that Outlaw has," May chimed in. "Remember when he threw you last week and ran off and we didn't know why?"

"Sure," said Jasmine. "My bottom is still bruised from landing so hard."

Corey's Pony Is Missing

"Well, we're never going to know what it was that scared him," May said. "We can love our ponies, feed them, take care of them, and ride them all we want. But there will always be things about them we can't know."

Corey thought about what May had said. It was true. Ponies were wonderful, but they weren't people and couldn't talk. They did keep secrets from their owners. That fact didn't make them any less wonderful. Even though she was a girl and Sam was a pony, they always had fun together.

"I kind of like that," said Corey. "But from now on, I want Sam's secret life to take place *in his stall*!"

"Lights out, girls!" Mr. Takamura said, peering around the edge of the door. "Time to go to sleep."

Obediently Corey turned out the light.

May scooted down under the covers and put her head on her pillow. She was remembering the drill practice earlier in the day.

"I think Max is up to something," she whispered to Corey and Jasmine.

"With all that drill stuff?" Jasmine asked.

"Yeah. He wouldn't have us working with Cross County without a reason," said May.

Pony Tails

"I bet you're right," said Corey. "Maybe there's going to be some kind of show."

"But why wouldn't he just tell us?" Jasmine asked.

"Maybe Max is just like Samurai," said May. "He likes to keep secrets, too!"

The Pony Tails giggled.

"Girls!" Mr. Takamura said from the hall.

"And if *we* want to have a secret life, we're going to have to whisper much more quietly!" Corey said.

And so they did.

COREY'S TIPS ON KEEPING
YOUR PONY SAFE

When your pony runs away, you quickly realize the importance of pony safety. Right after my pony, Samurai, came back, I got down to business on that subject, I can tell you!

I found out that there are two important parts of pony safety. The first has to do with keeping your pony from getting loose the way Samurai did. The second part has to do with making his home a safe place for him to stay.

Ponies are smart, really smart. A lot of them can figure out how to undo latches. People who use slide bolts on their stables often find their ponies running free. A pony can easily grab a bolt and move it until it opens, even if he has to lift it first. Trust me. If you want to find him in his stall every morning, use a bolt

101

with a clip on it. (May says I should use a combination lock on Samurai's stall!)

Next there's fencing. Sam loves to be out in the fresh air, but I'm never going to give him a chance to jump the fence again! My mother had the carpenter add another foot of fencing all the way around the yard, so it's now taller than I am. Max recommends adding an electrified wire to the top of that. I think it's a good idea, but Sam really is just a pony. He's a good jumper, but he can't go over five feet. He's safe in there now. Also, it's high enough that he can't get his head over it, and that means that he can't push against it with his chest.

Every time I'm standing by the fence, watching Sam or giving him a treat or just talking to him, I check the fence. If I ever notice that some of the slats or posts wiggle or move, we have it fixed. What starts as a slight wiggle can get to be a big wiggle quickly. A big wiggle can mean a quick exit for the pony if the fence falls down.

Oh, and the latch on the gate of the fence has a clip on it, too, just like the latch on the stall.

I'm always careful of the things in Sam's stall so that he's as safe there as he is secure.

Corey's Pony Is Missing

Nothing would be worse than to know that my own carelessness caused an injury to my pony. For that reason, I had the carpenter make sure the stall door goes all the way down to the floor. That way Sam can't get a hoof or ankle stuck under it. There's a bottom latch, too, so that he can't push the lower half of the door and get a hoof stuck.

The hook that holds his water bucket faces down and toward the wall so that there's no chance he'll catch his lip on it when he goes to take a drink. There is a manger for his feed, both grain and hay, so that it will stay clean and manure-free. I made sure there are no nails protruding from the walls of his stall that could scratch him or that he could get caught on. And there's wire mesh over the window on the inside of his stall so that he can't possibly break the glass and hurt himself that way.

There are also some things I do to protect the stable from fire. First, I keep it as clean as possible and never let junk like rags pile up. We have a little feed shed outside the stable to store grain and hay in. I clean Sam's stall daily and cart the soiled bedding and manure a safe distance away. And just in case, we have a fire extinguisher right by the door.

I respect Samurai a lot. I respect him

enough to know that he's smart enough to figure out how to get out of the stable or into trouble if I let him. I couldn't stand it if something else happened to him. Thank goodness he's safe and sound at home!

About the Author

Bonnie Bryant was born and raised in New York City and still lives there today. She spends her summers in a house on a lake in Massachusetts.

Ms. Bryant began writing about girls and horses when she started The Saddle Club series in 1987. So far there are more than fifty books in that series! Much as she likes telling the stories about Stevie, Carole, and Lisa, she decided that the younger riders at Pine Hollow, notably May Grover, have stories of their own that also need telling. That's how Pony Tails was born.

Ms. Bryant rides horses when she has time away from her computer, but she doesn't have a horse of her own. She likes to ride different horses and enjoys a variety of riding experiences. She says she thinks most of her readers are much better riders than she is!